AF308020

 tredition®

tredition was established in 2006 by Sandra Latusseck and Soenke Schulz. Based in Hamburg, Germany, tredition offers publishing solutions to authors and publishing houses, combined with world-wide distribution of printed and digital book content. tredition is uniquely positioned to enable authors and publishing houses to create books on their own terms and without conventional manu-facturing risks.

For more information please visit: www.tredition.com

TREDITION CLASSICS

This book is part of the TREDITION CLASSICS series. The creators of this series are united by passion for literature and driven by the intention of making all public domain books available in printed format again - worldwide. Most TREDITION CLASSICS titles have been out of print and off the bookstore shelves for decades. At tredi-tion we believe that a great book never goes out of style and that its value is eternal. Several mostly non-profit literature projects pro-vide content to tredition. To support their good work, tredition donates a portion of the proceeds from each sold copy. As a reader of a TREDITION CLASSICS book, you support our mission to save many of the amazing works of world literature from oblivion. See all available books at www.tredition.com.

Project Gutenberg

The content for this book has been graciously provided by Project Gutenberg. Project Gutenberg is a non-profit organization founded by Michael Hart in 1971 at the University of Illinois. The mission of Project Gutenberg is simple: To encourage the creation and distribu-tion of eBooks. Project Gutenberg is the first and largest collection of public domain eBooks.

A Short History of a Long Travel from Babylon to Bethel

Stephen Crisp

Imprint

This book is part of TREDITION CLASSICS

Author: Stephen Crisp
Cover design: Buchgut, Berlin – Germany

Publisher: tredition GmbH, Hamburg - Germany
ISBN: 978-3-8424-7921-0

www.tredition.com
www.tredition.de

A short
history of a
long
travel
from Babylon
to Bethel.
Stephen Crisp

INTRODUCTION

Writings of the first Quakers, even minor writings, often kindle in us today an ardor to seek what they sought and to find what they found. The excellent book by Luella M. Wright entitled "The Literary Life of the Early Friends, 1650-1725" is a pleasant and convenient introduction to these numerous and often lengthy productions of which 2600 have been listed for the first 75 years. Among them all, Luella Wright singles out one allegory; the only one, and it remained unpublished fully two decades after its composition. Why was this? Was it because, though the author was as sound a thinker and as persuasive an author as any among the followers of George Fox, an imaginary pilgrimage was inherently suspect, while the record of actual experiences in the form of a journal was not? Be this as it may, the slight loosening of standards with the opening of the eighteenth century allowed the "Second Day's Morning Meeting," which then censored Quaker manuscripts, to approve for printing "A Short History of a Long Travel from Babylon to Bethel." It was put out in 1711. How entertaining it would be to know the number of copies that were printed in that first edition.

Stephen Crisp was a famous preacher. "He had a gift of utterance beyond many" said his brethren in Colchester at the time of his decease. He was listened to by many outside the Society of Friends and his sermons, together with the prayer at the end of every one of them, were "exactly taken in character," that is in shorthand "as they were delivered ... in the meeting houses of the people called Quakers."

Though Stephen Crisp's letters, sermons, and journal promptly appeared in print and were widely circulated, the "Short History" remained after his death in the bundle of his papers in Colchester. John Bunyan's famous book "The Pilgrim's Progress" had appeared with its primitive woodcuts in 1678. It received immediate recognition and in due time was acclaimed the greatest religious book produced in England. Stephen Crisp's allegory is minimal besides it (some 30 pages as against 207), but the "Long Travel" retains significance because of its more modern point of view.

This tiny tract usually printed in pocket size (2" x 3") sometimes with a passage from the author's journal included, was reprinted more than twenty times. I happened upon it in the Friends Historical Library at Swarthmore College twenty years ago. They then had four copies. Today they have more than a dozen.

How does Stephen Crisp's theology differ from that of Bunyan's? In the first place, while Crisp's pilgrim starts off with a pack on his back of luggage for his journey, Bunyan's pilgrim had as his pack the burden of guilt which is original sin. Second, Crisp's pilgrim soon gives up confidence in human leadership having discovered a measure of the Light. Third, he crosses the river early on his journey, whereas for Bunyan's pilgrim the river is at the end, the river of death. Fourth, Crisp's pilgrim reaches the House of God in this life. He finds a satisfied multitude in the outer court. They invite him to stay with them in easy circumstances but catching sight of his guide, the Light, as it passes through a narrow door (compare Bunyan's wicket gate) he presses on, divests himself of his travel-worn garments and enters the House of God. Here, like the Friends with whom Stephen Crisp had found Peace after his own period of seeking, he first rests from struggle, then finds his calling which is to supply the needs of the young, and finally aspires to bring his good tidings to the Babylon from which he had set out.

"The Pilgrim's Progress" is incomparably more exciting with raging beasts, Giant Despair, and Apollyon with all his hosts. The people Bunyan's pilgrim meets are more vivid, portrayed with cruel detail and lusty humor. Theologically the Quaker tract is of a different age, not less exacting, but less pictorial. The medieval detail is gone but intense inwardness, devotion, and obedience are still required of the seeker to enable him to become a finder.

In his "Varieties of Religious Experience," which I heard William James deliver as a series of lectures at Stanford University when I was a Freshman over sixty years ago, he said of the religion of the Quakers: In a day of shams it was a religion of veracity rooted in spiritual inwardness and a return to something more like the original gospel truth than men had ever known in England. He continued, so far as our Christian sects are evolving into liberality, they are simply reverting in essence to the position which Fox and the early Quakers so long ago assumed.

With this conclusion I heartily commend to sympathetic seekers today the brief allegory by Stephen Crisp: "A Short History of a Long Travel from Babylon to Bethel."

Anna Cox Brinton

A SHORT HISTORY

In the days of my youth, when I lived at home in my father's house, I heard many people talk of the house of God; and that whosoever did attain to get into it did enjoy all manner of happiness, both in this world and that which is to come. And a great desire kindled in me, if it were possible, to get into the house; yet I know not where it was, neither did they who talked of it; but they had heard the report, and they reported what they had heard. There were also some books, that had been written by men who had been in that house; which books did declare much of the joy and felicity they had in the house. These books I got, and read them over and over; which did much strengthen my belief in the truth of the reports: yet by no means could I tell which was my way. But so ardent were my desires, that I thought myself willing to forsake my father's house, my country, and all, and travel anywhere, wherever my legs would carry me, so that I might find this house.

And upon a time, as I was breaking my mind to a friend of mine upon this subject, he readily told me, there were men appointed in every place to guide those who were willing to go thither, and it was their business, and they had nothing else to do. When I heard this I was comforted, and desired him, if he loved me, to make me acquainted with one of those men. He told me he would; which he did. When I came to treat with the man, I let him know the fervent desire I had to get to the house of God, of which I had heard such excellent things; and that I understood he was one appointed to guide any thither, who were willing to go, and to persuade people to go, who were not willing. He very readily answered, and told me, it was his business to guide any thither who were willing to go; and if I would comply with his terms, and follow him, he would lead me thither. I asked him what his terms were. He said the way was long, and would lead him from home, and I must bear his charges, and something over, to all of which I agreed.

So we set forward on our journey, early in the morning; but before we had gone one whole day's journey, I saw my guide sometimes stand still, and look about him, and sometimes he would pull a little book out of his pocket, and read a little to himself; which made me begin to mistrust that he knew the way no better than I.

However, I said nothing; but went on following him several days journey after this manner; and the farther we went, the more my guide was at a loss. Sometimes he went a little on, and then would look about him, and turn another way, and sometimes right back again for a while, and then turn again. So my suspicions grew very strong, and I began to be in great anxiety of spirit, but said little to him about it.

These books I got, and read them over and over; which did much strengthen my belief in the truth of the reports: yet by no means could I tell which was my way.

But one day, as we were travelling along, we met with a man that took notice of my sad countenance and tired condition. And he spake very kindly to me; "Young man," said he, "whither art thou bound?" And when I began to tell him something of my travel, he desired me to sit down upon the grass, in a shady place, and discourse a little about my journey: and so we did, and I told him how things had gone with me to that very hour. Whilst I was telling him my story, my guide fell asleep; at which I was not sorry, for thereby I had the more freedom to discourse with the man; and when I had told him all, he pitied me; and withal, told me, to his certain knowledge, this guide of mine had never been at the house, neither did he know the way to it, but as he had got some marks of the way, which he had received, as I or any other may do; and, if I followed him all my days, I should be never the nearer to it, and should find at last, I had spent my time, money and labour to no purpose.

This discourse did so astonish me, that I was at my wits end, and did not know what course to take. The man seeing what an agony I was in, began to comfort me, and told me that the house I sought was much nearer than I was aware of; and if I would forsake that guide, and follow him, he would soon bring me in sight of the house. "And," quoth he, "I am one that belongs to that house, and have done so several years. And whereas," said he, "thou art to bear his charges, and give him money besides, I will assure thee, it is not the manner of the guides that belong to this house of God, to take money for guiding people thither. I myself have been guide to many a one in my time, but never took one penny of them for it."

I
saw my guide sometimes stand still, and look about him, and some-

times he would pull a little book out of his pocket, and read a little to himself.

By this time, you must think within yourselves, how my drooping spirits were comforted; a new hope sprang up, and a resolution to forsake my wandering guide, and to follow this new one.

Upon which I awaked my guide, and told him my mind, and paid him what I had agreed for, and advised him never to serve any poor soul as he had done me: for I see, said I, thou knowest not the way, but as thou hast learned about it in some book. If book-learning would have served my turn, to find this famous house, I needed not thee, nor any body else to guide me to it; for there are very few who have written experimentally of it, but I have read them diligently: but now I have met a man that I judge has more experience of the way than thou hast, and I am resolved to go with him; and if thou wilt honestly confess thy ignorance, and go along with us, come and welcome; one guide will serve two travellers, as well as one in the way. But I could not persuade him; so I left him to take his own way as he pleased.

And he spake very kindly to me; "Young man," said he, "whither art thou bound?"

I now set forward with my new guide pretty cheerfully; and he entertained me with a good deal of discourse by the way. As he went on in pretty smooth paths, and without stopping, he told me, in a short time we should come in sight of the house; which made my travel easier. He also told me something of the rules and orders of the house, at which I was not at all discouraged; for I considered God was a God of order, and I doubted not but there were good orders in his house, to which I was willing to submit. And as we were thus travelling along, he of a sudden spake to me, saying, "Yonder is the house." At which I was exceeding glad; for now I thought I had not spent my labour in vain. The nearer we drew to it, the more my joy increased; and when I came in view of it, I pleased myself extremely with looking at it, and viewing the towers and turrets that were upon it, and the excellent carvings and paintings, with which it was adorned; and there was as much art in setting it forth as could be imagined. Oh! thought I, if there be so much glory without, surely there is more within, which I shall shortly be a partaker of.

As I was thus contemplating my happiness, and was come within as it were a bow-shot of the house, we were to go down into a valley; which we did: and in the bottom of the valley, glided along a small river, and I looked about to see a bridge to go over it, but could see none; at which I wondered; but on we went till we came to the river side; then I asked my guide where the bridge was. Truly, he told me, there was none, but we must go through it, and so must all that go into that house.

Upon which I awaked my guide, and told him my mind, and paid him what I had agreed for, and advised him never to serve any poor soul as he had done me.

I was a little troubled within myself; but he told me he had been through it, and there was no danger at all. With that I began to think within myself, have I taken all these pains, and shall I give over for so small a matter as this? What would I have gone through, when in my father's house, to attain to the knowledge of the house of God, and a possession therein? Not water, nor verily fire would have stopped me then, if I had so fair a prospect of it as I now have.

I told my guide if he pleased to go before, I would follow him: so in he went, and I after him; but when I came at the middle, there it was so deep that the water went over my head, but I made shift to keep my feet to the ground, and got well on the other side; and my guide and I went up together very pleasantly. When we came to the top of the hill, there was a wide plain, and in the middle thereof the house stood. So we went apace and drew near to it; and there I saw a very stately porch at the west end of the house, and at the door stood a strong tall porter, to whom my guide spake, and said to him on this wise: — "This young man hath long had a desire to be entertained in the house of God; thereupon I have conducted him hither." The porter asked him which way I came thither; he said, through the river: and I do not remember he asked me any more questions, but bid me welcome, and led me into the house, my guide going in with me, through many turnings and windings into a great hall. Mine eyes went to and fro as I went about the house; and in the great hall, there I saw many people, who bade me welcome, but none knew the anguish of my soul; for I began to question whether I was not again beguiled: for I found the house foul and dirty, in almost every part, and so belined with spiders and cobwebs, that I thought in myself it had never been swept clean since it was built. And some things I met withal that displeased me yet worse, as ye shall hear; howbeit, a good bed was provided for me to rest upon if I could; and I having little stomach, after I saw how it was made ready, went to bed, and disposed myself to sleep as I could. But, alas! sleep departed from me, and my spirits were grievously vexed, and my cogitations were many and grievous. Sometimes I thought of the paintings without, and how that suited not with the dirtiness that was within; and, if I was deceived, what course I should take.

The nearer we drew to it, the more my joy increased; and when I came in view of it, I pleased myself extremely with looking at it, and viewing the towers and turrets that were upon it, and the excellent carvings and paintings, with which it was adorned; and there was as much art in setting it forth as could be imagined.

After long and tedious thinking, I pleased myself with this: it may be better to-morrow. So I fell into a slumber a pretty while; but in the morning before I arose, I heard two or three contending about some accounts, in which one laid fraud to the other's charge; the other instead of vindicating himself, fell to twitting him in the teeth, with something of the like kind: they grew so hot in words, that one threatened to turn the other out of doors, and drive him back through the river, and never suffer him to come into the house any more.

was not again beguiled: for I found the house foul and dirty, in almost every part, and so belined with spiders and cobwebs, that I thought in myself it had never been swept clean since it was built.

My heart was ready to burst with sorrow; and in the anguish of my spirit I arose and went to them, and told them, I little thought to have found such doings, or heard such language, in the house of God. I fear, said I, I am deceived; and brought in amongst you by a fair show, but see not the glory, peace and tranquillity which I expected. So I walked away to another part of the house; where I heard a great noise and hard words; as I drew near, I understood it was about choosing an officer; and two were striving for it, and each of them had got a party, and each party grew hot against the other. As soon as I could be heard, I spake to them, and told them, such kind of doings as this, did more resemble a place in the world called Billingsgate, than the house of God. I went a little farther; and there I heard some women scolding about taking the upper hand, and about fashions in their clothes; and others about getting their children's play-things from each other. All this, and much more than I shall mention, increased my sorrow.

So I walked away to another part of the house; where I heard a great noise and hard words; as I drew near, I understood it was about choosing an officer; and two were striving for it, and each of them had got a party, and each party grew hot against the other.

I now began to long to speak with my guide that brought me thither; and with diligent search at last I found him, and began with him in this manner: Whither hast thou brought me? and where are the rules and orders thou toldest me were in the house of God? I have often read of the beauty, order, peace and purity of the house of God, but here I find nothing but the contrary. I fear thou hast brought me to a wrong house, and hast beguiled me. So I rehearsed to him what I had met withal; to which he replied; I must expect men to have their human frailties, and that men were but men: and he would have persuaded me to be satisfied, and make further trial. And as for the orders he spake of, they were mostly about meats and drinks, and about rules for electing of officers to rule the house of God; as I would see in time, if I stayed: and as to the dirtiness of the house, he confessed, that those to whom the care was committed to keep the house clean, had not been so diligent as they ought to have been; but he hoped, upon admonition, they would be more careful. To which I returned this answer: What! dost thou talk of human frailties in the house of God? That complaint is at large in the world, but doth not become the house of God; into which I have heard none can come, but such as are redeemed from the earth, and are washed from their pollutions; for God saith, all the vessels in my house shall be holy; and they that dwell in the house of God must have pure hearts and clean hands. And much more I told him of what I had heard and read concerning the house of God. I also told him plainly, I had let in such a belief of the peace, purity, glory and comeliness of the house of God, that I was persuaded *that* was none of it; and where to find it, I knew not; but if I never found it whilst I lived, I would never give over seeking, for my desires were after it, and I thought nothing would satisfy me short of the enjoyment of it. But as for your house here, said I, I have no satisfaction in it; it is not the place I seek for, so I must leave you. His answer to me was, he was sorry I could not be satisfied there as well as he; but if I could not, he would lay no restraint upon me: for his part, he had directed me as far as he knew, and he could do no more for me.

Several in the house threw things after me, in a spiteful manner, but none hurt me.

After our discourse was ended, I got up, and went out, but knew not where to go. Several in the house threw things after me, in a spiteful manner, but none hurt me. So I wandered sometimes north, and sometimes south; and every way that came in my mind. But whithersoever I went, the anguish of my soul went along with me; which was more than tongue can utter, or pen can declare, or any one can believe, except this relation should meet with some one that hath experienced the same travel; which, if it doth they will understand. But so it was, I had no comfort night nor day, but still kept going on, whether right or wrong I knew not, nor durst I ask anybody, for fear of being beguiled as before.

Thus I got into a vast howling wilderness, where there seemed to be no way, only now and then I found some men and women's footsteps, which was some comfort to me in my sorrow; but whether they got out without being devoured by wild beasts, or whither I should go, I knew not. But in this woeful state I travelled from day to day, casting within myself what I had best to do;—whether utterly to despair in that condition, or whether I had best to seek some other town or city, to see if I could get some other guide. The first I saw to be desperate; I also despaired of the last, having been so deceived from time to time; so that all these consultations did but increase the bitterness of my soul.

Thus I got into a vast howling wilderness, where there seemed to be no way, only now and then I found some men and women's footsteps, which was some comfort to me in my sorrow.

One day, as I was travelling in the afternoon, a terrible storm arose, with hail and thunder, and great wind, which lasted till night, and in the night also. And being weary, both of body and mind, I laid me down under a great tree, and after some time fell asleep. When I awaked and came to myself, it was still very dark; and, looking about, I saw a small light near me; and it came into my mind to go to it, and see what it was; and as I went, the light went before me.

Then it came into my mind, that I had heard of false lights, as *ignis fatuus*, and such like, that would lead people out of their way. Then thought I again, how shall I be led out of my way, that know no way of safety? And whilst I sat down to let these striving thoughts have their course, I took notice, and beheld the light as near me as at the first, as if it had waited for me. At which I was strongly affected, and thought within myself, maybe some good spirit has come to take pity on me, and to lead me out of this miserable condition. And so a resolution arose in my mind that I would get up and follow it, concluding in myself, that I could not be brought into a much worse condition, than I was now in. So I arose and followed it; and it went a gentle, easy pace at first, and I kept my eye straight to it. But afterwards, I found a great part of the luggage and provision I had got together, did but burden me in my journey; so I threw away one thing, and then another, that I thought I could best spare; but kept a great bundle of clothes still by me, not knowing whether I should need them.

And whilst I sat down to let these striving thoughts have their course, I took notice, and beheld the light as near me as at the first, as if it had waited for me.

As I thus went on, and the light before me, it led me out of the wilderness, along a plain country, without trees or inhabitants; only it appeared as if some few had gone that way;—and the light kept in that strait path, without any winding or turning, till I came to the foot of a great mountain; and, going up that mountain, I found it very hard getting up, and began to consider my large bundle of clothes and garments, and that several of them were of no use for a traveller as I was, that did not know how far I should go, nor whether I should want them, if ever I was so happy as to attain what I aimed at; nor whether the fashions would suit the place I was going to. So I threw away some, and anon other some, till none was left but what I wore.

Going up that mountain, I found it very hard getting up.

Thus, following my guide, I at last got up to the top of this mountain, where I saw another yet higher; I also saw a man that asked me whither I was going? I told him I could not well tell, but would tell whither I desired to go. He asked, whither? I said, to the house of God. He told me it was the way; but he thought I should never get there. I asked him, why? "Why," quoth he, "there are in yonder mountain so many vipers, adders, and serpents, and such venomous beasts, that they devour many people that are going that way. For my part," he said, "I also was going, but was so affrighted with those venomous serpents, that I was forced to turn back, and so would have you." I answered him, friend, I have for a pretty while taken yonder light to be my guide, and it hath directed me along this way, and I see it doth not leave me; look, dost thou see it there before me? He answered, "Yes, I see it." Well, said I, I have heard by travellers, that if a man have fire or light, the venomous beasts cannot hurt him; and I intend to quicken my pace a little, and keep as close to the light as I can. Come, go along with me and venture it. He said it was true, he had heard that fire would preserve from them, but he thought light would not; however, for his part he would not venture his sweet life amongst them; if I would I might; he wished me well, and so we parted.

I then made haste, and got pretty near the light, and up I went the second mountain; and when I came almost to the top of it, I saw many serpents' dens and vipers' holes, both on the right hand and on the left; and the venomous beasts drew near me, and hissed at me, and I began to be in great fear, and trembled exceedingly. But many times, when they were ready to sting me, the light would step in, or appear betwixt me and them, and they were affrighted, and ran away into their holes and dens.

saw many serpents' dens and vipers' holes, both on the right hand
and on the left: and the venomous beasts drew near me, and hissed
at me, and I began to be in great fear, and trembled exceedingly.

Oh! when I perceived this, how did my heart leap for joy within
me! My joy abounded,—my fear of the serpents abated,—my love
to my kind and tender guide increased,—and my courage and con-

fidence were renewed,—and I began to believe I was in the right way to attain my desire. So on I went, keeping my eye to the light through them all, without harm, till I came to the top of the mountain; and then I saw an exceeding large valley, so that I could not see the farther side of it: it seemed to be all moors, or places of water, and bogs and mire all over the valley, which began again to dishearten me; but, thought I, what shall I do? All is well hitherto. I was strangely delivered from the serpents; and whatever comes of it, if this light leave me not, I will follow it, if it be through fire and water.

So

that sometimes the light shined round about me, and I walked in the shinings of it with great fulness of spirit.

So I kept on, and went down the mountain, a gentle easy pace, and saw many of those cruel creatures by the way, who put out their stings at me, but none hurt me. And I took notice the nearer I kept to the light, the more they kept from me. So I got down to the bottom of the mountain, into the large valley, which was very green and pleasant for a little way; but by and by, the light went toward a great moorish ground full of water, and that I thought was very dangerous; but coming just to the side of the place, I saw a small narrow path through the middle of it, just broad enough for a man to go upon it; and into that narrow way the light led me, and went before me. Whilst I kept my eye steady to it, I went on safely: but if at any time I began to gaze about, my feet slipt into the mire and puddles; and then I had much ado to get into my way again. Had not the light kindly and tenderly waited for me, I had lost sight of it, and had perished in the way; for sometimes it was so far before me, that I could hardly discern it; and then I would quicken my diligence, and be more careful of my goings, and keep as close to it as I could; so that sometimes the light shined round about me, and I walked in the shinings of it with great fulness of spirit.

After a long time walking in this narrow way, I lifted up my eyes to the farther side of the moorish valley, and saw beyond, that there was a very high mountain, and on the top of it there was a great house: at the sight of which I was greatly comforted, supposing that might be the house I had for a long time sought.

For there were many who I perceived had been travelling in that narrow way, and had fallen into the mire; some on the right hand and some on the left, and they lay wallowing full of envy; some plucking at me, to pull me in; others throwing mire and dirt upon me to discourage me.

But after this I met with another sore exercise: for there were many who I perceived had been travelling in that narrow way, and had fallen into the mire; some on the right hand and some on the left, and they lay wallowing full of envy; some plucking at me, to pull me in; others throwing mire and dirt upon me to discourage me: others would speak very fair, on purpose to draw me into discourse with them, that whilst thus spending my precious time, I might be cast so far behind, as to lose the sight of my good guide. But I saw their evil designs, and was aware of them. So, keeping in my narrow way till I came to the end of the boggy valley, I then found firm ground under my feet, to my great comfort. I had gone but a little way, when my guide, the light, went into a narrow lane, well hedged on both sides; at which I was glad, thinking I could not go wrong, and need not now take so much care. But alas! I quickly found so many by-lanes, and ways, which lay almost as straight forward as that I went in, that if it had not been for the light, which went a little before me, I might certainly many times have gone wrong; but by carefully keeping to my good guide, I at last got up the mountain, and saw the house again. I then discerned a man of that country a pretty way off, and called to him, friend, ho! friend, what is the name of yonder great house? He told me the name of it was BETHEL. Then I presently remembered that that was the name by which the house of God was called in my father's country, where I had heard the reports of it, and so earnestly set out to find it.

Drawing nearer to it. I saw it had a large outward court, and a pretty large gate to go into it, so that a man might go in with a large burden on his back.

Oh! the joy and consolation that I felt in my soul, no tongue can express,—to think that now after all my travels, perils and disappointments, I had found what I sought for. So on I went, journeying with joy unspeakable; and as I went, I viewed the outside of the house: it was very large, and had but one tower; there was no carved work about it, no paintings, nor any kind of device that could be discerned; but all the stones were curiously joined together from the top to the bottom. I also took notice, that all the stones of the building were transparent, some more and some less; and I saw no windows to let in light from without; and, drawing nearer to it, I saw it had a large outward court, and a pretty large gate to go into it, so that a man might go in with a large burden on his back. So, coming to it, in I went; and there I saw many people that were very cheerful, and appeared to live very pleasant lives. Some of them told me, they had lived there many years, were well contented, and wanted for nothing; for there was a mighty tree grew in the midst of the court, and the fruit thereof was good, and the leaves also, and it bore fruit all the year long. And many of them were so kind as to invite me to sit down and eat with them; but that I refused; and they showed me a great cistern, which they had hewn out to themselves, to catch water from the elements; and they had made themselves convenient lodgings in the sides of the court, to lodge in.

And when I was stripped stark naked as ever I was born, I tried to enter, and found no great difficulty.

But all this did not satisfy me; for I saw my beloved guide pass through them all, and enter in at a little narrow door at the farther side of it. Whereupon I left them, and made haste to the door, where I saw my guide had entered; and I attempted to enter in thereat, but could not, it was so strait; which put me in great sorrow of mind, and what to do I knew not; my thoughts troubled me on every side, and all ways I tried, but in vain. Oh! thought I, are all my troubles and labours come to this? Must I be shut out at the last? What shall I do? As I was thus perplexing myself, I thought I heard a voice, but knew not from whence it came, which said, "Young man, strip thee of thy old garments, and so thou mayest enter." This occasioned yet more trouble of mind; for I was loth to go naked: but at last thought it better to go in naked, than not at all. So I at last fell to stripping, thinking that a few pitiful rags should not hinder me of so great an enjoyment.—And when I was stripped stark naked as ever I was born, I tried to enter, and found no great difficulty; and so soon as I was entered, one met me, and cast a garment of pure white linen over me, which reached to my feet; and he brought me into a narrow room and said, "Rest here awhile." Then I lay me down in so much joy and comfort as is impossible to be expressed; all things were so pleasant about me, and my resting place was so delightful, and my heart was so fully satisfied, that it overcame me with songs of joy. But I found it my business to be still and quiet in my happy condition, that I was come to enjoy.

As I was entered, one met me, and cast a garment of pure white linen over me, which reached to my feet; and he brought me into a narrow room and said, "Rest here awhile."

I had not been long in this room, before I was called out to see the beauty and comeliness of the house. As I walked through it, I found every thing so clean and bright, that I was ravished in an admirable manner. I also met with some people that welcomed me to the house of God with such kindness as refreshed my heart: and as I came to be acquainted with them, I marked their conversation, and their discourses were exceedingly comfortable to me; no quarrelling, no contention, no high nor hot words, but all passed with meekness and reverence, and due respect one for another. The young men waited for the words of the ancients, and the virgins carried a reverent respect to the matrons; and there was an universal concord and unity, so that I wondered greatly. One day as I was opening my mind to an ancient, I told him I admired much, and wondered greatly at the universal concord that I had taken notice of, beyond all I had met with in my life. He said it must needs be so, and could not be otherwise, for that was the guide to lead me hither, which had been the guide to them all. And further told me, there could be no contention, but where two spirits strove for mastery; but it was not so in this house. His answer was so full and satisfactory to me, that I said no more to him at that time, but went on viewing, and beholding the order of every thing I saw, till my soul was filled, and I might say my cup did overflow. So that my former labours and disappointments, sorrows and perils, did signify nothing to me, having now a full reward, an hundred fold.

Then he that talked with me, told me it was my work to teach the children so far as I knew, and had learned, and as far as I should from time to time be further instructed.

So I returned to my rest again, in a larger room than before, singing praises to my God, and setting forth the praises of the house, and of them that dwelt therein. And awhile after, I was called forth from the room where I was, and told I was not brought to that place only to take pleasure and delight therein; but there was work to be done, and I must take my part of it, and be faithful and diligent in my employment, to which I answered, it was enough that I had attained my desires in being admitted into this heavenly place; but if there was any business that I could do, I was willing to do it, be it what it would; for it would be my greatest joy to do anything to the advancement of the honour of the house of God, and them that dwell therein. Then he that talked with me, told me it was my work to teach the children so far as I knew, and had learned, and as far as I should from time to time be further instructed. I was a little amazed thereat, knowing my inabilities: but having a little pondered that part of the sentence, that I should be from time to time further instructed, I took courage in my work, and made some progress in it, with great fear and reverence; waiting daily for those instructions I was to receive, and which I did receive in an abundant manner; and the work prospered in my hand, and the children loved me, and I loved them entirely, as though they had been my own children: and many of them grew up to a good understanding, and observed their places and orders to my great delight.

And let none of them say, it happened better with me than with many; for I have understood, since coming into this house, that the same Light that appeared to me, doth appear to any poor distressed soul in the whole world.

After I had thus continued a while, he that talked with me came and told me I must take the charge of part of the household, and give them their meat in due season; and suit every one's meat, in dividing to every one's state and condition, and not feed strong men with milk, and babes with strong meat; for which purpose he gave me a key that led into the treasury or store-house; which, when I came to see and behold, was abundantly filled with all sorts of nourishments, that never could be exhausted, or spent, while the world endured. And I observed that whatever I and others took out to distribute daily among the household of God, the store-house was still full as at the beginning, and so continues to this day, and forever.

And now, having continued a long time in this heavenly habitation, it comes into my mind to let my countrymen, and the children of my old father, whom I left in Babylon, hear of me; for I suppose they judge me lost or devoured; but I could be glad if any, yea, all of them, were here to behold, and taste and feel what I do. And let none of them say, it happened better with me than with many; for I have understood, since coming into this house, that the same Light that appeared to me, doth appear to any poor distressed soul in the whole world; but the reason that so few come here is, because they fear the perils and dangers that are in the way, more than they love the Light that would lead them through them; and so turn aside, and shelter themselves in an old rotten building, that at one time or other, will fall on their heads, and they perish in the ruins.

So I went not, but sought a city whose builder is God; and now I have found it; Hallelujah in the Highest; glory, honour, and renown to his worthy Name and power, throughout all ages and generations. Amen.

Now if any have a mind to know my name, let them know I had a name in my father's country, but in this long and tedious journey I have lost it. But since I came hither I have a "new name," but have no characters to signify it by, that I can write, or they can read. Yet if any will come where I am, they shall know my name. But for further satisfaction, I was born in Egypt, spiritually called; and my father went and lived in Babylon, about the time the true children of Israel were in captivity; there I became acquainted with some of the stock of the Jews, about the time they were returning to their own land; and they told me wonderful things of the glory of the house they had at Jerusalem, and would have had me go with them. And I understood that Solomon, with many thousands of carpenters and masons had built it; upon which I considered within myself, that if Solomon and the carpenters and masons had built it, carpenters and masons might at one time or another pull it down again. So I went not, but sought a city whose builder is God; and now I have found it; Hallelujah in the Highest; glory, honour, and renown to his worthy Name and power, throughout all ages and generations. *Amen.*